C.D. Clues

by Anne Miranda
Illustrated by Luisa D'Augusta

Scholastic Inc.

New York   Toronto   London   Auckland   Sydney

Copyright © 1998 by Scholastic Inc.
Scholastic Phonics Chapter Books in design is a trademark of Scholastic Inc.
All rights reserved. Published by Scholastic Inc.
Printed in the U.S.A.
ISBN 0-590-03078-7

4 5 6 7 8 9 10   14   04 03 02 01 00 99

Dear Teacher/Family Member,

Scholastic Phonics Chapter Books provide early readers with interesting stories in easy-to-manage chapters. The books in this series are controlled for sounds and common sight words. Once sounds and sight words have been introduced, they are repeated frequently to give children lots of reading practice and to build children's confidence. When children experience success in reading, they want to read more, and when they read more, they become better readers.

Phonics instruction teaches children the way words work and gives them the strategies they need to become fluent, independent readers. However, phonics can only be effective when reading is meaningful and children have the opportunity to read many different kinds of books. Scholastic Phonics Chapter Books cover many curricular areas and genres. They are carefully designed to help build good readers, but more importantly, to inspire children to love reading.

Contents

1 ★ A Creepy Story

"Look," said C.D. Clues. "The new people are here."

Suzy peeked out the window and looked down the street. "How do you know?" Suzy asked.

"I'm a detective," said C.D. "I know all. I see all."

C.D. was Suzy's brother. He called himself "C.D. Clues." He said he was the best detective in the town of Cross Creek.

"I hope they have kids," said Suzy. "Can you see that, too?"

"They have three kids," said C.D.

"How do you know?" asked Suzy.

C.D. said, "Let's go and see if I'm right."

Mom, Dad, C.D., and Suzy went to meet the new people. There were three kids. There were twin boys and a girl named Carly who was just Suzy's age. C.D. was right, three kids.

C.D. showed the boys his treehouse. Suzy and Carly hit it off and the two girls played all day.

When it was time to go home, Carly said, "Do you think your mom would let you sleep at my house?"

"Let's ask," said Suzy.

Suzy's mom talked to Carly's mom and they made a plan. It was getting dark, so C.D. walked the girls to Carly's house.

"BOO!" said C.D. as they went down the street.

The girls jumped a mile.

"Don't do that," said Suzy.

"Your imaginations made you jump," C.D. told them.

C.D. left the girls with Carly's mom. Soon Suzy and Carly dashed up to Carly's room, but they couldn't sleep.

"Let's tell creepy stories," said Carly. "I like creepy stories."

"I know a creepy story," said Suzy. "Once there was a big green monster with big green teeth. It was walking along, and it came to a little monster's house. The big green monster tapped on the window. 'GIVE ME THE BOX,' it said. But the little monster would not open the window."

Just then—something tapped.

Carly jumped. "There's something in here!" she yelled.

"It's your imagination," Suzy said.

Just then, something tapped again.

"Something is in here," said Carly, "and it's not my imagination."

Suzy jumped this time. "Turn on the light so I can see what it is," she said.

Carly turned on the light. "I don't see a thing!"

Then something said, "GIVE ME THE BOX, GIVE ME THE BOX."

Something was in Carly's room. Was it the big green monster?

2 Was It a Dream?

Suzy screamed. Carly screamed. The screams were so loud that C.D. could hear them at his house. He ran to see what happened.

Tears streamed down Carly's face. She could not speak.

"I want to go home," said Suzy.

"I feel creepy," said Carly at last.

"You have a great imagination," said Carly's mom. "Maybe you were having a bad dream."

"The tapping and talking were real," said Suzy. "Carly didn't dream it. I could hear it, too."

"I think you need a detective," said
C.D. "Can I help?"

Carly's dad said, "OK. See what you
can do. Carly's mom and I will be here if
you need us."

"I want to see and hear for myself,"
said C.D. Suzy held C.D.'s hand, and so
did Carly. They went up to Carly's room.

"Tell me what happened," said C.D.

"When I was telling Carly a creepy
story, I could hear something tap," said
Suzy. "I could hear it speak. It said,
'GIVE ME THE BOX.' That was just what
I had said when I was telling the story."

"That's odd," said C.D. "It speaks? It
said part of the story? Great! That
gives me a lead."

C.D. looked all over the room and on each shelf. He peeked under each bed.

"I don't see a TV or anything that could talk," said C.D.

Just then, something tapped. C.D. jumped. Suzy and Carly jumped.

C.D. put his hand up to his ear to hear. "That's another great lead!" he said. "The something is not in the room. It's outside and it wants to get in."

"Just like the big green monster!" screamed Carly.

C.D. peeked out the window. "I see something in the tree," he said.

"Is it green?" asked Suzy.

"I think so," said C.D.

"With big teeth?" asked Carly.

"No," said C.D. "It has a beak."

"A monster with a beak?" asked Carly.

"It's too small to be a real monster," said C.D. "I think it's a bird."

"GIVE ME THE BOX. GIVE ME THE BOX," said the something.

"Did you hear it?" asked Suzy. "So that's it. It's a talking bird!"

"Well, Mrs. Green used to live here. She had a talking parrot," said C.D. "I bet that it's hers."

"I have some seeds for my parakeet," said Carly. "I'll get some for the parrot. Maybe it will come in to eat them."

"Neat," said Suzy.

Carly got the seeds, and C.D. opened
the window. When Suzy held out her
arm, the parrot landed on it and began to
eat the seeds. One by one, the parrot
seeds popped into its beak.

"Mrs. Green went to live in another
state. I wonder how her parrot found its
way back," said C.D. "How, how, how?"

"Don't you know all? Don't you see all?" asked Suzy.

"Well, I may never know how the parrot got here, but I do know what to do now," said C.D. "Mrs. Green must be in tears over her lost parrot. Maybe we can send her dear parrot to her on a plane."

"What a kind thing to do," said Carly.

"We will need a big, clean cage and a box," said Suzy.

"GIVE ME THE BOX. GIVE ME THE BOX," said the parrot.

They all smiled.

"Great!" said Carly.

"What a good team we make," said Suzy.

3 We Are a Team

C.D. Clues was a great detective. He was also a great gardener. Last year, he won three first prizes for his vegetables at the Cross Creek Garden Contest.

This year, C.D. and Suzy worked as a team and planted a garden. C.D. planted seeds in neat rows and watered them. Suzy weeded. Their garden was neat and clean and green.

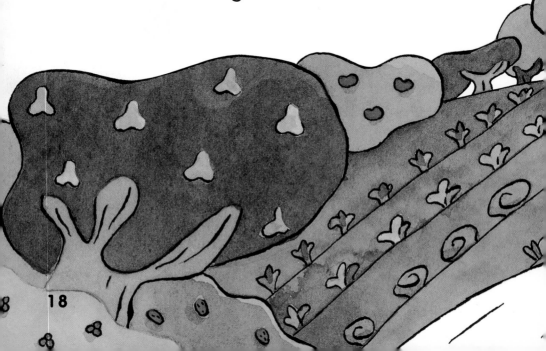

"Suzy, I think we should win first prize," said C.D.

Suzy smiled. She liked that idea.

One morning, the sun was bright. It would be a great day for gardening. Suzy pulled on Mom's old green boots. The boots were too big, but they kept Suzy's feet clean. She went into the garden.

"My beans, my green peas, my beets!"
Suzy screamed.

Suzy ran up and down the neat rows in
Mom's old green boots. Something had
eaten most of the vegetables.

C.D. came running up to Suzy. "What
happened?" he asked.

"It's our vegetables," Suzy said.
"Something has eaten them."

"But what?" asked C.D. "We need to
look for a lead."

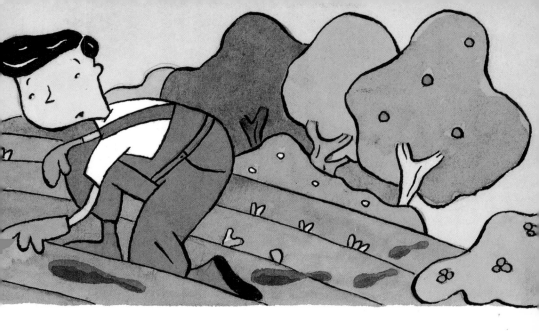

C.D. looked up and down the neat rows and took notes. Then at last he said, "He or she has on big rubber boots."

Suzy tapped C.D. "Look at my feet. That was me," she said.

"I'm not thinking right," he said. "I'm too upset. How are we ever going to find out what happened?"

"I have a plan. We can camp out tonight to see if it comes back," said Suzy.

"Great idea," said C.D.

That night, Suzy and C.D. put up Dad's old tent by the garden wall. Suzy got into her sleeping bag. Then C.D. and Dad got into sleeping bags, too.

"We should take turns sleeping," said C.D. to Suzy. "You go to sleep first."

"Good idea," said Suzy. Soon she was sleeping and dreaming of winning a prize. Dad went to sleep, too.

C.D. sat in the tent. "I'll be up so I can see if something creeps into the garden," he said to himself.

But soon C.D. began to feel sleepy. He wanted to stay up, but in a wink he was sleeping, too.

In the morning, when Suzy woke up, she screamed, "My green peas, my sweet corn!"

C.D. leaped out of his sleeping bag.
He looked around.

"You were sleeping!" said Suzy.
"You should have seen what happened.
Someone has come in and eaten the
vegetables again."

C.D. looked down. "I see," he said. "But now we have a lead."

Suzy saw the prints between the rows. "Those are odd feet," said Suzy. She bent down to look. "It's not a rabbit. It's not a dog. It's not a cat. I think it's a deer."

"We should check," said C.D.

They went to get a book about animals. She was right. It was a deer.

"You are getting to be a great detective," said C.D.

"That's me!" said Suzy.

4 ★ Oh, Deer

"The deer must have needed food. It came all the way to our garden to eat," said Suzy. "Once deer find food, they will come back again and again."

"Oh, dear," said C.D. "We don't want the deer to get into the garden again. The garden contest is less than a week away."

"We should make a fence," Suzy said. "That should keep the deer out once and for all."

"Good idea," said C.D.

C.D. and Suzy got some wood and sticks and began to make a fence. They worked all day.

"We made a great fence," C.D. said.

"Let's sleep in the tent again to see if the fence keeps the deer out," said Suzy.

"OK. But this time, I'll be the one who sleeps first," said C.D.

That night, C.D., Suzy, and Dad got into sleeping bags again. Soon C.D. and Dad were sleeping. Then Suzy felt sleepy. In a wink, she was sleeping, too.

All of a sudden, C.D. gave her a shake. "Wake up," he said. "Our fence didn't work. We didn't keep the deer out. We kept the deer in."

Suzy saw the trapped deer. The deer didn't have a lot of room to run inside the fence, so they couldn't jump out.

"We need help," Suzy said. "Let's call a forest ranger."

Suzy and C.D. went into the house, and Mom made the call. Soon the ranger came by in a big green truck. He looked at the deer trapped in the garden.

"That's a great deer trap," said the ranger. "It worked well."

"But we didn't mean to trap the deer," said Suzy.

"We wanted to keep the deer out of the garden," said C.D.

"Well, it's not safe for the deer to stay here. I must take them back to the forest outside Cross Creek," said the ranger.

The ranger put down the back of the truck. "Come and help me steer the deer into the truck."

The deer walked out of the garden and into the ranger's green truck. The ranger took them deep into the forest where they would be safe and have food to eat.

Suzy and C.D. looked at their garden. It was a big mess.

"I am glad the deer are OK," said Suzy, "but I wish our garden was, too."

"Don't feel bad, Suzy," said C.D. "If we don't win a prize this year, we can try next year, too."

"Once again, you are right," said Suzy. "How do you know so much?"

"I know all. I see all," smiled C.D.

Suzy smiled, too.

Decodable Words With the Phonic Elements

1 **ee**

Creek	sleep
creepy	street
green	teeth
meet	three
peeked	treehouse
see	

2 **ea**

beak	neat
clean	real
dear	screamed
dream	speak
each	streamed
ear	team
eat	tears
hear	
lead	

3 **e**

be
began
he
me
she
we

4 **review**

e	ea	ee
be	dear	Creek
he	eat	deep
me	mean	deer
she	year	feel
we		green
		keep
		need
		see
		sleep
		sleepy
		steer
		week